The Four Faces of God

Adapted from the teaching of

Ian Clayton

Printed in USA, UK and New Zealand
ISBN No. 978-1-911251-31-6

Acknowledgements

Son of Thunder Publications would like to thank Ian Clayton for his teaching and consultation in this book.
We would also like to thank Revelation Partners for the story and Patricia Ford for assistance.

Our special thanks goes to Maryam Kurowski for the paintings in this book.
Instagram *@maryamsworldofart*
Contact: *maryamsworldofart@gmail.com*

Adam is upset.

Adam misses
his dad.

Adam sees
stairs he has
not seen
before.

At the top of the stairs he sees a shining curtain and goes in.

Adam feels excited in this good place.

He sees the face
of a kind Ox.

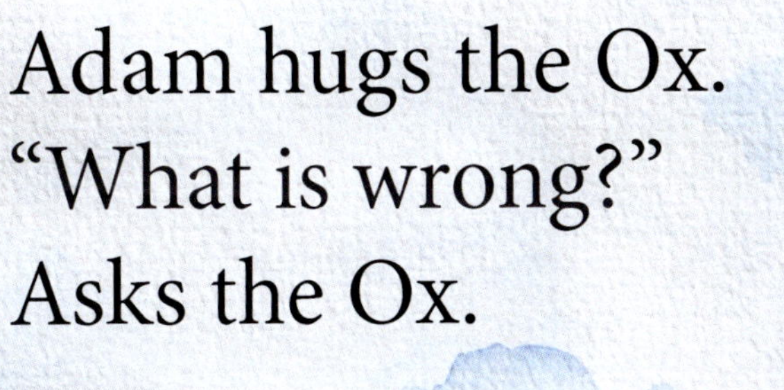

Adam hugs the Ox.
“What is wrong?”
Asks the Ox.

"I miss my dad"
says Adam.

“I know” says the Ox. I will work on your heart and your dad’s heart to make them soft again”.

“Do you want
to fly with my
friend Eagle?”
Asks the Ox.
“Yes!” Says Adam
with joy.

Adam flies on Eagle's back in the sky. He sees the River of Life with a waterfall and a rainbow over it. Adam is very happy!

“I never want to go back” says Adam.
“Why not?” Asks Eagle.
“I am scared” says Adam.

My friend Lion will give you strength.

Adam meets the good Lion. This Lion is full of love and power.

“What is wrong?” Asks Lion.
“I don’t want to go back” says Adam.
“I will fill your heart with love and power!” Roars Lion.

Adam is full of peace and love.
“Thank you Lion” he says.
“Your home is good again” says Lion, “I am in your heart and will be with you every day”.

Adam is happy.
He goes back
home.

“Adam!” Says Daddy. I love you, I’m sorry I was upset.”

“I love you too Daddy” says Adam.

Four Faces of God

Coloring Book

Adam misses
his dad.

The shining curtain

Adam meets the ox

Softening hearts

Flying on the eagle's back

Adam's heart filled with love

Going home

Wrapped in the arms of love

Draw your own